'TOMO... Is a Great Word

written

by

Janeen Brian

Produced by Martin International Pty Ltd
[008 210 642]
South Australia
Published in association with
Era Publications, 220 Grange Road, Flinders Park,
South Australia 5025

Text © Janeen Brian 1991
Cover design Steven Woolman 1991
Printed in Hong Kong
First published 1991

All rights reserved by the publisher.

National Library of Australia
Cataloguing-in-Publication Data
Brian, Janeen, 1948-
    'Tomorrow' is a great word.

    ISBN 1 86374 006 6 (giant bk.).
    ISBN 1 86374 007 4.

    1. Readers (Primary). I.Title.
    (Series : Magic bean junior novel).

428.6

Available in:
Canada from Vanwell Publishing Ltd, 1 Northrup Crescent,
       PO Box 2131 Stn B, St Catharines, ON L2M 6P5
New Zealand from Wheelers Bookclub, PO Box 35-586
       Browns Bay, Auckland 10
Singapore from Publishers Marketing Services Pte Ltd
       10-C Jalan Ampas, #07-01 Ho Seng Lee Flatted Warehouse,
       Singapore 1232
United Kingdom from Arncliffe Publishing, Roseville Business Park,
       Roseville Road, Leeds LS8 5DR

MY DIARY

INTRUDERS BEWARE I BITE!

Name: Louisa E. Cordone

Address: 515 Short Ave.

Glenelg

South Australia 5045

Telephone: 124 987

Birthday: April 4th

LOVE IS ~~GREAT~~

WILD!

~~PAIN~~

Stupid!

LC
4
ED.

Eddie ||||| ||||| ||||| ||

Leon ||||| ||

April 14

Dear Diary,

Today I'll give you a name 'cos I reckon it'd be boring just being called 'Diary'! Okay, next letter after D is E. You can see I've got brains, can't you? What about Eddie, Eliza, Ebenezer, Einstein, Edwina? Maybe just E.

Well, E, had a rotten day. Leon is a . . . Tut! Tut! No swearing. Leon is a <u>fink</u>. In the hall talking to Kate *all* lunch hour. Huh! True love stinks! Carolyn sent this crazy note with a drawing of our geography teacher, Mr Graham, all around the class and we added bits to it. So funny!

Then stupid Kate bursts out laughing. 'Course old Graham gets hold of it and wham! We all get kept in at lunchtime. Thanks heaps, Kate.

Home — note from Mum and Steve.

Dear Louisa,

Steve and I have picked up Michael from school and gone shopping in the city. Might be late. Heat up spaghetti for dinner. Hope your tennis practice went well.

love Mum xxxoooxxx

P.S. Louisa, will you please put the garbage out? Thanks, Steve.

P.P.S. Did you feed Fish and Chips today?

Jeeze! I told them there was no more tennis practice! And they tell *me* off for not listening! Now I'm stuck here. Lucky I've got you, Diary, er, E! No one else. Sorry, Fish and Chips, but I don't speak goldfish language. Did anyone ever tell you you've got it easy, just swimming round and round, no one picking on you, no fights, no pimples!!!! No offence, Fish and Chips, but you're not the most exciting pets a girl could have. Can't put a leash on you and take you for a walk! Not like Benjy. Beautiful old dog.

But now, we're stuck here, in Steve's apartment. 'NO PETS ALLOWED'. So Steve buys me fish for my birthday!

Wish we were back in our old house, just Mum, Dad, Benjy, Michael and me. No, forget Michael. Buy him a one-way ticket to the Moon! I'm never getting married and I'm never having kids. I'm just going to have a big house in the country with lots of dogs and cats and horses and cows and a pet goat and a pet lamb. And I'll have apple trees and yummy peaches and plums and I'll grow some vegetables (NOT SPINACH!!).

Anyway, here I am, bored out of my pizza brain and Steve writes, 'Did you feed Fish and Chips today?' I've only forgotten twice! I can't help it if fish are so quiet and . . . forgettable! And then, 'Put the garbage out'. It's always *me*, never Michael. 'Why don't you try to get on better with Steve?' That's Mum. 'Michael does.' Well, bully for Michael the wonder boy. But I don't want to go fishing with Steve. I hate seeing fish caught with hooks in their mouths.

Why did Mum have to marry again anyway? Oh, well, at least I didn't have to move schools. THE ONLY GOOD POINT!

April 15
Dear E,

Sallyanne reckons she can fit

19 olives in her mouth. We're going to try and beat the record this weekend. Melanie can fit 102 pieces of popcorn. So she says! But Melanie can levitate. SO SHE SAYS!

April 16
Dear E,

Wish Dad hadn't moved to another city. He never made me do anything I didn't want to. Now Steve says, 'We're a family and we have to help each other'. Which means I do all the work! Who does he think he is anyway, my real dad? Well he's not and he never will be! AND, just because Michael's a bit older (only 2 years), he only does the dishes two nights out of seven.

UNFAIR! SEXIST! UNCOOL!

April 17

Dear E,

English homework tonight. Make up a joke. TRUE! I could just copy. Mrs Jacobs wouldn't know. Here, E, some for you (copied).

Q: What is a forum?

A: Two-um plus two-um.

(HA! HA! HA!)

Q: Why did Santa Claus plant a garden?

A: Because he wanted to hoe! hoe! hoe!

(YUK! YUK! YUK!)

(Strictly for those still putting baby teeth in glasses of water)
Stay here. Just going to get an apple and a sandwich. Probably a million calories!!

Okay, now a joke written exclusively by the famous Louisa:
Er . . . Er . . . Er . . . (so far, so good, eh? Just wait till the punch line, it's even funnier.)
What did the dog say. . .
Why did the helicopter try to . . .
Why did the caterpillar jump . . .

Mum's gone shopping again today. I'll do it later. Wish I could have gone. They've got jeans on special and I could have shown her.

They're great, they've got patterns on the top of the pockets. Sally-anne's got some. *IF* I'd gone shoppi

oh my God   where am I?
what's happened   its dark
can't see   blackness   Did I pass
out? frightened   head   aches

can't move my leg   painful
crushed   everything sharp
poking into me   blackne

donn't know where I am up to on

the page use my   finger hold the
page shift finger down   each time
my leg   must be blood everywhere   sticky can't breathe
face full of grit   choking
where am I

think I'm here on page
pressed hard with fingernail
last time

wish I could turn   sore
mouth dry   tried to think

what happened   accident?
earthquake? bomb?   am
I dreaming

remember now   room shaking
window rattled   Fish's and Chips'
bowl crashed   books everywherr
sce screaming   dived under bed
noises   loud   terrifying
after that   nothing

E, I'm frightened I'm alive but
think I'm buried   been hours I
think

hard to breathe   whats going to
happen *why me!!!* why didnt Mum
remember about tennis pracrtice?
I would have been with them —
not here   *WHY!!!*

darkness   silence   wherre am
I feel sick vomit am I going to die
here   *I DONT WANT TO DIE !*

 yelled yelled   silence   no one
knows   Mum and Steve must
know!! where are you? dust
sneezed   body hurts   leg bad
have to tie something around it
ripped dress   for bandage

E   dont want to move what if
eveything falls down have to move
so stiff

leg pressing cold metal think its
leg of my bed feels like it

hope so!

 bed!   sloping like a roof   must
have stopped me being crushed to

death
 remember! torch under mattress
have to find out!
        cant move to get to mattress —
      big piece of wood jammed in
      the way
  loosened wood!   something
crashed   missed my head able to
get further under bed   torch

16

Dear E,

Hallelujah!! I've found the torch, trouble getting it though! (kept it under the mattress for late night visits to the toilet and for late night reading!)

Can't believe my luck. My heart is pounding now that I can see. Oh, wonderful, wonderful torch! It's like a bomb site here—thick dust, broken metal, wood, bricks, bits of walls, everything broken and jammed. If it weren't for the bed, I would have been killed. My leg is swollen—a big gash, bigger than I thought — so much blood — it throbs painfully all the time. I'm thirsty—still have the apple in my jacket pocket (eaten the sandwich, bad luck) had a small bite—put the rest on a bit of wood—a shelf?? Not much room, about as big as a double bed . . . can only sit up, not stand. Feel like a dog in a kennel.

We were on the second floor. Lucky old Mrs Henstridge below us was away.

What about the other apartments? What about *me?!*

Dear E,

I don't want to turn the torch off. Have to soon. Not sure how long batteries will last. Can't bear the thought of darkness again —

always frightened of darkness — remember poster of Red Riding Hood and the Wolf in my bedroom when little — I was terrified the wolf would leap out of the picture and get me as soon as it turned dark — always wanted the hall light left on.

Dear E,

What can I do? My leg is so sore and puffy—there's pus too, so I think it's infected. Knocked it a minute ago when I tried to turn. Pain was unbearable. What if I try and put splints either side and bandage it like you do for snake bites? Will that help? At least that way I might not knock it as much. It'll be harder when I go to the toilet though. It's hard enough now! I try and scratch a bit of a hole but it's b . . . awkward! Then I cover it with a brick or lump of concrete, whatever — feel like a dog — so dirty. I tie a strip of my dress on to a small bit of wood and shove it where I've been, like a flag — but there's not much room, and it stinks. I just use anything to wipe my 'you know what'.

Dear E,

What a clever girl I am! Dragged a blanket from the bed. More comfortable all bunched up to sit on. And when I wrap it around me, I get a feeling that everything's going to be all right.

I think of my family and home. Yelled and yelled and YELLED! Someone will find me.

Dear E,

Heard a noise, a scratching sound, like a mouse or cricket. Hoped it was someone. Yelled and yelled.

Saw it! A tiny, brown mouse! Nibbling at the apple. Couldn't believe my eyes. Now I know everything will be OK. Something else is alive down here.

Dear E,

The mouse ran away. I'll bite off small pieces of apple for him. I name thee, oh mouse, Sir Liberty!

Dear E,

I'm so thirsty. Liberty crept up to a piece of apple I left on the shelf. I waited and waited. Hardly breathed. He's so little! And his whiskers twitch all the time. He ate the whole apple piece!

How long have I been here??? Can't tell time. My watch was smashed. Please, someone, come! Mum, Steve, PLEASE FIND ME!

Dear E,

Still here.

Roast lamb, mint sauce, baked potatoes, chocolate pudding and chocolate sauce and ice-cream.

This is a list of my birthday food. Steve cooked it for me (not the ice-cream!) No present yet from Dad. Probably busy at work. He's got a really important job— and a girlfriend. Hope I like her.

Dear E,

Re-read entry on April 14th before the earthquake (was it an earthquake?) If not, what else?? Never had one in Adelaide before, that I know of.

Come to think of it though, dear old Geography Graham did say the Para Fault Line ran through our district. Huh! How come I get low marks for geography and I remember things like that!

Still re-reading April 14th. Don't know what I ever saw in Leon. Think I only wanted to see if I could get him. He always talks about himself anyway. KATE — if you're out there somewhere — you're welcome to him — with bells on!

Dear E,

Saw Liberty. He nibbled another piece of apple. I made it

smaller. I might need it more than him! Feel very dizzy. Leg in sort of splints. How much longer?

Dear E,

Don't sleep much, don't dare, have nightmares. What if everything fell and I was crushed? I scream, but feel weaker, throat drying up. Lips cracked. Know about dehydration. Mum told me that people have drunk their own wee to stay alive. Will I? Could I? I feel sick thinking about it.

Dear E,

Is it day or night? Wish my wristwatch was working. Never

thought of it being so important
to me.

Dear E,

Desperate for Liberty to stay.
When he disappears I am so alone.
Already he comes closer for his bit
of apple.

Dear E,

What is happening!! Is there
life out there?!

larry

Dear E,

Have I told you about my pet
guinea pig, Larry, that I had when I
was little? Can't remember what
I've written. Can't waste batteries

going back to find out. Anyway, he was black and white and very furry. Then 'he' became 'she' and had four babies. We gave them away. Then Larry got sick and she died— in front of me. I kept trying to make her move even though she was dead. I built a cross and buried her in the garden, but I kept wondering what I had done to make her die. I felt sad. Dad said he would buy me another, but he never did. I think grownups should keep their promises, don't you, E?

Dear E,
    No-one has come!

Dear E,

Sometimes I can't think straight, can't remember the names of some of the kids in my class! Is there still school? I even miss that!

Think of Mum and Steve and Michael all the time. Are they alive? If they are, why haven't they found me! What if they're not? Oh, please, make them alive.

Dear E,

Hardly move at all now. Took splint off—pain all through leg—twice the size of the other. Is it rotting?

Dear E,

Steve says when we have more money we're going to buy a house and I can have pets again. He sat on my bed one night when I'd been crying and told me that.

Dear E,

If I get out alive, I promise I won't tease Michael about his girlfriends and I won't send them letters with his name forged at the bottom. Come to think of it, I wouldn't have liked that either. Especially not to Leon! Also, Michael, I'm sorry I smashed your butterfly collection, but I hated the way those beautiful creatures were lying there stabbed with pins, in a box in your drawer—in darkness. They should be outside and free. I know you were studying them but it looked cruel. Still they weren't mine. I shouldn't have done it.

Dear E,

Just thought of Fish and Chips. Hope they died quickly and didn't suffer.

E, now I know why Steve bought Fish and Chips for me for my birthday. He knew how much I was missing Benjy and hated moving from our big home to his place. They were the only pets he could give me (besides a bird, I guess) but I didn't understand. I thought it was a dumb present. I didn't even say thank you.

Dear E,

I want to hear Mum laugh again.

Dear E,

Please let me see my family! And I want to ride to school with Sallyanne, finish the novel I was reading, see the big, blossom tree at the side of the building and run along the beach again! I want to be able to grow up.

Dear E,

Going to try and get out. So dizzy, which direction?

Dear E,

Tried to pull out slabs of concrete above the bed.   More stuff fell down   terrifying more dust grit in my mouth battering choking   no air

Later—tried again   another landslide. Hole getting smaller cramped   what else can I do? Hopeless must   rest

Dear E,

Did the landslide scare Liberty away? I need him to talk to and to hold—try to catch him.

Put last piece of apple under bowl held up with stick, waited and waited — felt like hours. He crept under bowl—pulled stick away, got him. Hooray!

E,

I killed him! Heard strange cries   lifted bowl a bit   cries stopped.   Liberty was dead bowl must have hit side of head. Liberty I'm sorry. Total despair. Oh God, I'm so alone!

Have to get out! How? Please — please someone help me.

Do I dig? or sit and wait? I yell—I scream—isn't any sound getting out? Isn't <u>anyone</u> looking for me??

DUGGAN SCHOOL

Must get out   must   must
don't want to die   must get out
   trapped   must
death wolf will get me

I'll get out not far can't be far I'll
do it   take bit by bit   slowly stay
calm   calm oh, God, don't let
everything crash Mum where are
you? keep hearing your voice

 no food   apple gone   need drink
desperate   want to scream
        GET OUT!!!! panic sweating
scratching at things   nails and
hands bleeding   musnt sleep
heard loud noise   felt shaking

PLEASE, not a cave-in!!

   have to take a chance   so far
shifted leg of chair   brick   part
of fireplace (I think) and

E! batteries are fading! have to
work quicker! stuff falling everywhere   batteries!
        E,   batteries have gone   no
    more light   world has ended
    darkness   throat and mouth
    dry can't swallow   can't go
    on   can't do it — butterfly in
    darkness   tired   no use
    what have I written E? stuff I
dont want anyone to see ? dont
know   I dont know anymore.

At least Liberty died quickly

E, banged on leg of bed with torch like morse code what's the use

E, felt for photo of family   cried can hardly write its the end must make a will

Mum — crystal necklace that she gave me on the day she married Steve   my books and photo album

Steve — photo of Benjy and me in brass frame   my Home Economics Cookery book

Michael — Benjys collar

money in bank book to buy
new butterfly collection

Dad—portrait of me when I was 4
my school reports

Sallyanne—my diary, E.

Sorry for all the times Ive
been a pain   love you all
E, everything in my will   is it all
smashed—will I ever be found?

is *this* my grave?

E, thankyou for being a friend
pain everywhere   so tired feel
weak now   time to go   wish I
        knew if family are alive
perhaps I'll get to see my pet
        guinea pig andLiberty
is there a pet section in heaven?

            is there a heaven?
whatever

Dear E,

I'll start a brand new page. Thought you'd like to know I'm alive! Amazing, isn't it? I'm tucked up in a hospital bed, Bed 17, Ward 5E, to be exact. There's a vase of yellow roses from Mum and Steve on my side table and the smell is beautiful. I take great gulpfuls — I'm greedy for the perfume.

There's a fax from Dad (quickest thing he's ever done!) and a plane ticket to visit him during the next school holidays. I'm sure it's my birthday present, though he didn't exactly say so and there was no birthday card—but it's a great present anyway.

Wonder if he'll have a moustache or not when I see him. His moustache is black and when I was little, I asked him what it was. He said it was a caterpillar, so one day when it wasn't there, I asked him what had happened and he said it had turned into a beautiful butterfly and flown off. I believed him for months . . . until he grew another moustache!

Anyway, where was I? Oh yes, and there's a present from Michael too. He was so embarrassed when he gave it to me. What do you think it was? A chain with a tiny, silver tear-drop on it. Michael had cried too. Wow!

That's pretty special . . . but he said I can only show Sallyanne (if I have to) and noone else. Fair enough.

How can I tell you what it's like to be alive? IT'S GREAT!!!

I'm really looking forward to walking again. The doctors reckon about another three or four days, and then with crutches. My leg was pretty bad. Sometimes I still feel the pain. There'll be a scar, but that's nothing. I just want to be outside and smell the fresh air.

I've got a drip in my arm — I was badly dehydrated when they found me. Steve says it may take a bit of time to get back to my FILM-STAR GOOD LOOKS,

(Michael says it will take forever!) and he's promised to bake roast lamb with mint sauce again, the day I get out of hospital. What a pal!

Guess what? Mum's got a new job—administrator of a child care centre — more money too, so that means we'll be able to get a house sooner than we thought.

'Course Steve's place is gone and almost everything in it, including our photo albums. Lucky I'd kept the family photo in you, E! Everyone's staying at Aunty Jo's until everything's sorted out.

Well, E, that just about brings you up to date—except for one thing.

I've just read my entry about heaven —it's hard to believe how close I was to death. I still don't know if there is a heaven, but if there is, it couldn't be much better than where I am at the moment!

Mum has told me most of what happened. Our building went down like a pack of playing cards and so did all the other buildings and houses in the area (and the blossom tree). It was chaotic—a freak earthquake—we hadn't had one before (so, Mr Graham, you'll be happy to know I do learn something in your classes!).

When my family finished shopping, it was late. They felt the 'quake where they were on the other side of Adelaide, but only heard the news of the damage on the car radio. They rushed home (what was left of it) but of course I was nowhere to be seen.

After several days, the police and rescue workers told families that it was unlikely they would find any more survivors. But Mum and Steve wouldn't give up looking.

They refused to believe that I was dead. Mum kept pleading that the search go on. (So that's where I get my stubbornness from, eh, Mum?!)

They must have been ex- hausted. I've seen the mountain

of stuff they had to shift from the photos that Steve took. Oh, and that noise I'd heard, it wasn't a cave-in, it was the hydraulic rescue equipment!

Anyway, Mum figured out that I would probably have been in the kitchen ('food' being my middle name) or the bedroom when the earthquake struck, so that narrowed it down. The first clue Mum had was when she saw the leg of my bed. (That bed should be cast in gold!)

Even then she didn't know if I was there or not, or whether I was alive, but she suddenly caught sight of me through a hole in the wreckage, as they moved rubble.

I was leaning under the bed, unconscious, but still holding on to you, E. They quickly organized an ambulance and oxygen . . . and the rest is history. I was trapped for a total of 6 days, 1 hour and 35 minutes!

I'm a bit tired now, so I'll sign off, till tomorrow.

(E, isn't 'tomorrow' a great word!)

47

OTHER BOOKS BY AUTHOR JANEEN BRIAN

PICTURE BOOKS
Down They Rolled (Magic Bean, 1987)
Mr Taddle's Hats (Magic Bean, 1987)
Andrea's Cubby (Magic Bean, 1988)
Fables — A Short Anthology (Keystone/Magic
Bean Classic, 1991)

NONFICTION
South Australia's Early Colonial Years (Hodder &
Stoughton, 1985)
The Flemings of Hopetoun (Brian, 1989)

POETRY ANTHOLOGIES
My Sister Learns Ballet (Omnibus, 1984)
Putrid Poems (Omnibus, 1985)
Petrifying Poems (Omnibus, 1986)
Vile Verse (Omnibus, 1988)
Four and Twenty Lamingtons (Omnibus, 1988)
Off the Planet (Omnibus,1989)
Fractured Fairytales and Ruptured Rhymes
(Omnibus, 1990)
Christmas Crackers (Omnibus, 1990)
Stay Loose, Mother Goose! (Omnibus, 1990)